GO A WAY MONSTER SPRAY

JENNIFER GIORNO-BRENNAN

MINDSTIR MEDIA

Published by Mindstir Media, LLC
45 Lafayette Rd | Suite 181| North Hampton, NH 03862 | USA
1.800.767.0531 | www.mindstirmedia.com

Printed in the United States of America
ISBN-13: 978-1-7354785-2-4

For my parents,
Louis and Carolyn Giorno

Brittany was a happy little girl who loved her Mommy, tumbling, climbing, jumping, baking cookies, and making faces at her little brother, JJ.

Nothing scared her: not big dogs, not boys, not cabbage. Not even a thunderstorm! She was fearless!!

But then....one night....Brittany had just settled down under her covers when she heard it!

THUMP! BUMP!

"I'm not scared," she whispered.

CREAK! SQUEEK!

She put her fingers to her ears.

"I'm NOT scared," she said a little louder.

BOOM!

"MOMMY! Mommy!"

Mommy rushed into the room. "What's the matter, Peanut?"

Brittany shrieked, "Monsters! Monsters in the hallway! I heard them THUMP and BUMP!"

Mommy smiled, "I just came from the hallway. I didn't see any monsters."

Brittany took a deep breath. "They came into my room! I heard the CREAK and SQUEEK."

Mommy looked around.

"The-the-", Brittany gave a sob. "The CLOSET!" They went into the closet. I heard the THUMP and BUMP!

Mommy wiped Brittany's tears and gave her a hug. "Do you want me to check everywhere?"

Shaking her head and covering her eyes, Brittany said, "Oh no Mommy! I don't want to see. And DON'T open the closet. The monsters might get out. Maybe they will eat me and JJ!"

Mommy checked the closet from top to bottom, the hallway from end to end, and under the bed again and again. Mommy reassured Brittany that everything was fine, but Brittany asked her to check just one more time.

No matter how many nightlights, "monster checks", or reassuring words, Brittany was sure the monsters were lurking every minute!

Mommy thought and said, "In the morning I'll check my Mommy Handbook to see what it says about getting rid of monsters."

Brittany sniffed, "Okay, but will you stay with me until I fall asleep?"

"Of course", Mommy said as she layed down next to Brittany.

The next morning Brittany came into the kitchen for breakfast. Mommy stood at the counter. "I have something for you that will help with those nasty monsters," she said with a big smile. She stepped aside and Brittany saw a spray bottle.

Mommy held it up. "See? This is Go Away Monster Spray. All you need to do is shake and spray anywhere you think the monsters might be at bedtime."

Brittany frowned, "It doesn't look very strong."

"Oh it is," Mommy said proudly, "I made it myself."

"Okay, I'll try it tonight." Brittany went into the playroom to play with JJ. Secretly she asked JJ, "Do you think that spray will work? I don't think it will." JJ just giggled.

That night, after her bath, and after putting on her favorite nightgown, Brittany stood in the doorway of her room with Mommy by her side and grabbed the Monster Spray. Mommy read the back of the bottle aloud.

Brittany shook the bottle vigorously and said, "Get ready to run, monsters!" She sprayed her closet from top to bottom, the hallway from end to end, and under the bed again and again. And again.

Then, without hesitation or any fear, Brittany leapt into bed, said her prayers, kissed her Mommy goodnight and told Mommy to turn off the light! She kept her Monster Spray right next to her...just in case she needed it in the middle of the night.

But she didn't need it.

Not even once.

The next night, she didn't need to hold her Mommy's hand, and sprayed all by herself. The night after that, Brittany didn't spray the closet, just the hallway and under the bed. The next night, she sprayed just under the bed. And then, one night, she didn't need to spray at all, she felt the monsters were gone for good. But...she kept her Monster Spray in the back of the closet.....just in case.

The Monster Spray stayed waaay in the back of the closet, gathering dust, until one night... Brittany was reading a bedtime book to her Mommy when all of a sudden, JJ yelled, "Mommy! Mommy! I heard a THUMP and a BUMP and a SQUEEK and a CREAK!"

Mommy started to get up, but Brittany said, "Stand back, Mommy, I got this!"

Brittany fumbled in her closet and went waaaay in the back and found her Monster Spray. She looked at her Mommy and explained, "I'll read this to JJ and help him like you helped me. You can come and listen if you want, but I get to read it to JJ and help him spray, ok?"

"OK", Mommy said smiling.

"It's ok, Peanut, I'm here", Brittany said.

Mommy's heart was filled with love and joy as she watched Brittany wipe her brother's tears, give him a hug, hold his hand and read the Monster Spray label aloud, just as Mommy had done for Brittany!

DIRECTIONS TO MAKE GO AWAY, MONSTER SPRAY

- Grab an empty spray bottle

- Fill it 3/4 of the way with water

- Add a sweet smelling essential oil to repell monsters

- Add another essentail oil for courage

- Mommy blows into bottle 3 times to add her love and protection

"Oh, how I regard the new and fragile courage born from a child's brave and wondrous imagination. For without fear, there can be no courage."

Jennifer Giorno-Brennan

AUTHOR BIOGRAPHY

Jennifer Giorno-Brennan began her thirty-two year elementary school teaching career in 1985 after graduating with honors from Temple Universtiy with a Bachelor of Science in Education. She is a second generation educator and retired in 2019. Reading to her students' was her favorite part of her teaching career. She is a wife and proud mother of two grown children, who are the inspration for her writing. Jennifer is a member of NJREA and SCBWI.

CPSIA information can be obtained
at www.ICGtesting.com
Printed in the USA
BVHW022243281020
592102BV00014B/65